Sienna
the Saturday
Fairy

For Plum Tilley,
with lots of love and fairy magic

Special thanks to

Sue Mongredien

ISBN-10: 0-545-06761-8
ISBN-13: 978-0-545-06761-4

12 11 10 9 8 7 6 5 4 3 2 1   8 9 10 11 12 13/0

Printed in the U.S.A.

First Scholastic printing, August 2008

Sienna
the Saturday
Fairy

by Daisy Meadows

SCHOLASTIC INC.

New York   Toronto   London   Auckland   Sydney
Mexico City   New Delhi   Hong Kong   Buenos Aires

The
Fairyland
Palace

Time
Tower

Windy
Lake

Tippington
Town

Morristown
Aquarium

The Tall
Toy
Store

Fashion
Fur

Fountain

Dancing
Days

Town
Hall

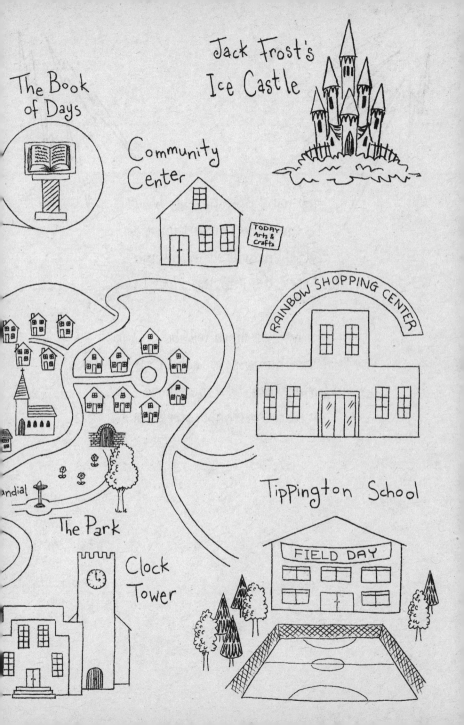

Icy wind now fiercely blow!
To the Time Tower I must go.
Goblins will all follow me
And steal the Fun Day Flags I need.

I know that there will be no fun,
For fairies or humans once the flags are gone.
Storm winds, take me where I say.
My plan for trouble starts today!

Contents

Fantastic Fashion

"You look beautiful," Rachel Walker said, looking at her friend Kirsty Tate.

"So do you," Kirsty replied. The two girls grinned at each other. Kirsty was staying with Rachel during their school vacation, and they'd been doing all sorts of fun things together. But today, Saturday, was going to be especially

exciting. Rachel's cousin, Caroline, was opening a new clothing store in the Rainbow Shopping Center. Caroline had planned a fashion show featuring some of the store's cutest clothes. Even better, she had asked Rachel and Kirsty to be two of her models!

"There," said Anna, the stylist, as she gave Rachel's French braid a last squirt of hairspray. "You two are ready. You'd better find Caroline and get your first outfits on now. The show starts in fifteen minutes."

Kirsty and Rachel thanked Anna and jumped down from their swivel seats. They were in the makeup room, which was part of the temporary backstage area behind the stage.

Just then, Caroline appeared in the doorway. "Hi, girls," she said. "You both look great. Let me quickly show you around before the show begins."

Kirsty and Rachel followed Caroline, both feeling tingly with excitement. The fashion show was going to take place in the lobby of the mall. There was a backstage area with large screens and partitions that made different rooms, and it seemed like a maze. "First, I'll show you the stage," Caroline said. The stage

was long and narrow, with lots of bright
spotlights — just like a real catwalk!

There were two hidden entrances. As
the girls peeked out from behind the
curtains backstage, they saw a
cameraman setting up his equipment.

"He's from the local paper," Caroline
told the girls. "Hopefully we'll get a

picture in the *Gazette*. It would be amazing publicity!"

Kirsty and Rachel could see that some people were already sitting in the rows of seats on either side of the catwalk. Unfortunately, none of them looked excited to be there. In fact, most of them seemed a little bored!

"The mood is kind of flat," Caroline said, looking around with a puzzled expression. "Hopefully, once the rest of

the audience arrives, everyone will be a little more excited."

Rachel shot Kirsty a look. Both girls knew exactly why the audience looked so down — it was because the Saturday Fun Flag was missing!

Kirsty and Rachel were good friends with the fairies. The girls had been called to Fairyland many times to help out. This time, Jack Frost had stolen the seven Fun Day Flags and taken them back to his ice castle. Without the flags, the Fun Day Fairies couldn't make the special magic they needed to spread fun around the human world. Now everyone was just plain miserable. But Jack Frost's goblins had had so much fun with the Fun Day Flags that they had grown mischievous and had started playing

pranks — even on Jack Frost himself. Jack Frost eventually lost his temper and cast a spell that sent the flags to the human world. So far, Rachel and Kirsty had helped the Fun Day Fairies find five of their flags, but there were still two left to find — including Saturday's!

"Now, the wardrobe room is right over here," Caroline said, striding down the hallway. Caroline led the girls through a doorway into a large room crammed with racks of clothes, hats, shoes, and accessories.

"Wow!" Rachel exclaimed as she gazed around.

"You'll be wearing three outfits each," Caroline explained. "They're all here, with your names on them." She pulled out three hangers marked "Rachel" and three marked "Kirsty." Then she gave the girls boxes of shoes to match their outfits. "You can get ready in here," she said, showing them into a small dressing room nearby.

She checked her watch. "You've got ten minutes to change into your first outfits before you need to be on stage."

Kirsty and Rachel hung up their clothes as Caroline rushed off. The first outfits they had to wear were party dresses with fancy strappy shoes.

"This is so cool," Kirsty said, slipping into her long, silvery dress. "Will you zip me up please, Rachel?"

Rachel helped Kirsty, then put on a floaty pink dress and matching necklace. "This is going to be so much fun, even without the Fun Day Flag," she said. "But I hope we can find today's flag before those horrible goblins do!"

Rachel and Kirsty knew that they weren't the only ones looking for the Fun Day Flags. Jack Frost's goblins had really missed the fun of the flags, so they escaped from Fairyland into the human world to find the flags again.

"Girls, you look fabulous!" came a voice from behind them.

Rachel and Kirsty turned to see Susan, Caroline's business partner. "Come to the stage with me. You two are the first on," she said, smiling. "Try and relax! Imagine you're at a real party when you're out there," she  advised the girls as she led them toward the catwalk.

Susan guided Rachel to the entrance on the right of the catwalk and showed Kirsty the entrance on the left. "When I

give you the cue, I want you to walk out
onto the stage and meet in the middle,"
she said to them both. "Then you can
walk down the main aisle together.
When you reach the end, you turn and
walk back up and out through your stage
entrances. Got that?"

Kirsty and Rachel had just enough
time to nod and take their places as the
music started.

Susan winked at them. "You're on,"
she said. "Off you go!"

Fun on the Catwalk

Kirsty walked onto the stage, feeling nervous. The lights were dazzling, but her favorite song was playing. She stepped forward in time with the beat, and soon found herself grinning. This was fun!

But then Kirsty looked down at the audience and nearly stumbled when she

saw the gloomy expressions on some of
their faces. One person had even fallen
asleep!

Kirsty and Rachel walked toward each
other and went the rest of the way down
the catwalk together as Susan had
instructed. "We've got to find the
Saturday flag!" Rachel hissed out of the
corner of her mouth. "Nobody's having
any fun!"

Kirsty nodded. Rachel was right. They needed fairy Fun Day magic to put some sparkle into the show!

The girls had reached the end of the catwalk now, so they spun around and walked back the way they'd come. A tiny pattering of applause followed them. Once offstage, they exchanged worried glances.

"Where could the flag be?" Kirsty wondered as they returned to the changing room.

Rachel shook her head. "I don't know, but remember what the Fairy Queen always says? We shouldn't look for the magic, because it will come to us."

"I know," Kirsty said, gazing around the changing room. "I just hope it comes to us before the end of the fashion show!"

The next outfits that the girls had to wear were part of the store's winter collection. They had coats, boots, hats, gloves, and scarves to put on over warm sweaters and wool pants. Quickly, Kirsty pulled on her sweater and pants, and then took her coat off its hanger. As she did, she let out a gasp. "Rachel, look!"

Rachel turned to see, and then she gasped, too. A bright pink scarf hung under Kirsty's coat, but it wasn't an ordinary scarf. It was fuchsia, with a sparkly sun pattern in the middle of it. Rachel realized immediately that it was the Saturday Fun Flag.

"The magic *did* come to us!" Rachel declared with a grin. "Fantastic!"

Kirsty tied the flag carefully around her neck. "I'll keep it safe until we can find Sienna the Saturday Fairy," she said.

Rachel nodded. "And then she can take it back to Fairyland and recharge her wand," she agreed happily.

The girls knew that the Fun Day Flags served a very special purpose. Every morning in Fairyland, Francis the frog, the Royal Time Guard, went to the Time Tower to check the Book of Days and find out which day it was. Then he selected the correct Fun Day Flag and ran it up the Time Tower flagpole. All the while, that day's fairy waited below in the courtyard with her wand held

high. When the sun's rays hit the
glittering flag, a stream of magical
sparkles reflected off it and beamed
straight into the fairy's wand. The
sparkles charged the wand with special
Fun Day magic.

"The sooner Sienna recharges her
wand, the sooner this audience will cheer
up!" Kirsty added.

But then Rachel
frowned. "You
have gloves, but
I don't seem to
have any," she
said to Kirsty.
"I wonder if I
should have some,
too. I'll go and check
with Caroline."

Kirsty nodded. Rachel left her friend to
finish getting dressed as she rushed out of
the room.

"Oh yes, you should have gloves,"
Caroline said, when Rachel found her.
"Where could they have gone?" She
started rummaging through the wardrobe
room, trying to find them.

"Any luck?" Kirsty asked, appearing in the doorway a few minutes later. She had her full winter outfit on now. "Susan just gave me a two-minute warning. That's when she needs us on the catwalk again," she added.

"Here they are!" Caroline said at last. She pressed a pair of pale blue gloves into Rachel's hand.

"Thanks," Rachel said. "See you in a minute, Kirsty. I'll be as quick as I can!"

Rachel rushed back to the changing room, but she discovered that the rest of her outfit was missing now! She stared around in disbelief. Everything from her hat to her boots had completely disappeared. "Oh no!" she cried. "Where is everything?"

Just as the words left her mouth, a burst of bright pink sparkles streamed from one of the gloves in her hand. A tiny, smiling fairy peeked her head out.

Rachel recognized her immediately. "Sienna!" she exclaimed in relief. "I'm so glad to see you!"

Goblin Grab

Sienna the Saturday Fairy had long
brown hair that was tied in thick pigtails.
She wore a fuschia top with a pink
pleated skirt. A pink star necklace
sparkled at her throat, and dainty red
ballet slippers were laced up her ankles.
She smiled at Rachel. "Sorry," she said,
"I think it was my fault that your gloves

were missing. I cast a spell so that I would appear inside one of them, but I think the magic made the gloves pop up in a different place!"

"I'm just glad you're here," Rachel assured her. "Guess what? Kirsty already found your flag!"

Sienna's eyes shimmered with joy. "I thought it would be around here somewhere. That's just what the new poem in the Book of Days said this morning," she declared. Then she recited aloud:

"Hats and scarves and coats and shoes,
The flag you'll find, but then you'll lose.
Do not despair, remember this:
The fashion show is where it is!"

"Speaking of the show," Rachel said anxiously, remembering what she was supposed to be doing. "I should be onstage modeling a winter outfit any minute, but all the clothes are missing!"

"Don't worry," Sienna said, twirling her wand between her fingers. "If you tell me what you were supposed to be wearing, I can work some fairy magic for you."

Rachel smiled thankfully. "It was a thick white coat, with a fur-trimmed hood," she said, "a pale blue scarf and hat, and big, white, furry boots."

Sienna waved her wand, and a flurry
of pink sparkly fairy dust swirled around
Rachel. Moments later, she was fully
dressed in all the right clothes.

"Thank you, Sienna. That's perfect!"
Rachel laughed. "Now I'd better go."
Sienna nodded and hopped into
Rachel's coat pocket as Rachel rushed to
the stage.

"OK, girls, you're on!" Rachel saw Susan say to Kirsty, who was at the right catwalk entrance. But when Rachel looked over to the other entrance, she stopped in her tracks. There was a different model getting ready to step onto the stage — wearing her outfit!

"Why would anyone steal my outfit and pretend to be me?" she whispered to Sienna, feeling confused. She peeked out of the entrance as Kirsty and the other model both set off down the catwalk. She

could see that the people in the audience
were starting to perk up now, no
doubt because the Saturday
flag was on stage nearby.
Kirsty was smiling at
them, not realizing
that it wasn't
Rachel who was
next to her.

From
backstage,
Rachel looked
closely at the
model who had
taken her place. She
saw that the model had
a very long, pointy, green
nose. "It's a goblin!" she yelped
in horror.

Sienna stared in disbelief. "A very tall goblin," she whispered anxiously. It was true. The goblin was at least twice as tall as he should have been. And now he was reaching a warty green hand toward the scarf around Kirsty's neck! "He's after the flag," Rachel cried in dismay. "We've got to stop him!" She hurried out onto the catwalk, determined to warn Kirsty that there was a goblin on stage.

At the same moment, Kirsty reached the end of the catwalk and did her twirl. As she looked back down the way she had come, she saw that there were two Rachels, dressed exactly the same on stage with her.

Kirsty gasped in surprise, and then her eyes narrowed as she realized that one of the Rachels was a goblin. Before she could react, the goblin lunged toward her. He snatched the Saturday Fun Flag from around her neck and raced back down the catwalk.

Cloaked by Clothes

"Hey!" Rachel cried, seeing the goblin
running down the catwalk toward her
with the flag. She tried to stop him, but
he tripped her. Poor Rachel went
sprawling onto her hands and knees!
Kirsty ran over to help her friend get up,
but by that time the goblin had
disappeared off the stage.

Rachel's cheeks were flushed. "Let's get off the catwalk so we can find that goblin," she said to Kirsty in a low voice. Together the friends marched quickly back down the catwalk. The audience members were smiling and clapping — luckily, they seemed to think it was all part of the show!

Susan was waiting for the girls as they came off stage. "Are you all right?" she asked in concern. "I saw that you'd fallen, Rachel, but I didn't see how it happened. I was getting Emma ready," she explained. She motioned toward another model who was now heading down the catwalk. "And then I looked around and saw you in a heap. Did you bump into each other?"

"Something like that," Rachel said. "But I'm fine now, don't worry."

"Glad to hear it," Susan said. "Take
a few minutes to sit down and recover.
I'll rearrange the order of the models
for final outfits, so that you two are the
last on. That way, you can catch
your breath."

"Thanks, Susan," Kirsty said. But as
soon as they were
out of sight,
Kirsty and
Rachel looked
at each other.

"There's no way
we can sit down and
rest now," Rachel said seriously.

"Not when we have a Fun Day Flag to
get back," Kirsty agreed. "I can't believe
that goblin just snatched it. How are we
going to tell Sienna?"

"Don't worry, Kirsty," Sienna said, popping her head out of Rachel's pocket. "I saw the whole thing, and it wasn't your fault."

Kirsty jumped at the sound of Sienna's voice. "Oh, hello," she said, smiling sheepishly. "I'm glad you're here, Sienna, but I'm sorry about your flag."

Sienna fluttered out of Rachel's pocket and flew over to Kirsty. "It's all right," she said. "I guessed something like this might happen after I read today's poem." Then she recited the poem again for Kirsty.

"*Do not despair, remember this: The fashion show is where it is,*" Kirsty repeated thoughtfully when Sienna had finished. "So the flag's still here somewhere."

Sienna nodded.

"Look," Rachel said, as they walked past a pile of clothes on the floor. "That's my outfit!"

"And a pair of stilts!" Sienna said,  pointing them out to the girls. "That's why the goblin looked so tall." She waved her wand, and the pile of clothes and the stilts magically vanished.

The girls and Sienna hurried back to the wardrobe room, and Rachel pushed the door open. "Let's start looking in here, okay?" she suggested. "There are lots of places for a sneaky goblin to hide."

Kirsty and Sienna agreed, and the three friends crept into the room together. There were so many racks of clothes to search through that they all started looking in a different place.

Kirsty skimmed through a rack of long evening gowns — but there wasn't anybody hiding between them. Sienna waved her wand, and a whole row of hats flew off their pegs and up into the air, but there wasn't anybody hiding underneath them.

Meanwhile, Rachel was flipping through a long rack of coats when she suddenly spotted a pair of knobby green knees that were poking out from under a toddler's yellow raincoat. When she looked more closely, she could see a corner of bright pink fabric showing, too. It was the goblin and the Fun Day Flag! Rachel tiptoed toward him.

Goblin in a Spin

At that very moment, the goblin peeked out from between the coats and saw Rachel coming toward him. With a cry of alarm, he darted away.

"I found him! He's somewhere around here!" Rachel shouted to Sienna and Kirsty, and she squeezed through the coats to chase after the goblin.

Kirsty rushed over to help, and Sienna
fluttered up into the air.

"I think I saw him in that corner,"
Sienna called to the girls, pointing with
her wand.

"There he is!" cried Kirsty, spotting a
large green ear that was poking out from
behind a black dress. But once again, the
goblin ducked away before the girls
could reach him.

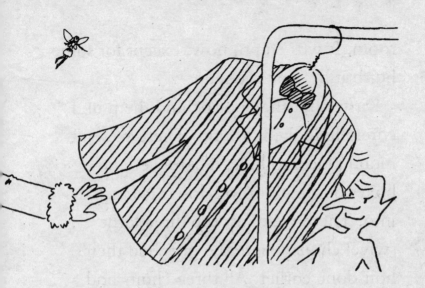

Rachel followed the sound of his footsteps and caught sight of his long nose sticking out of a man's suit. She made a lunge for him, but the goblin bounded away just before her fingers grasped the flag. This time, he dashed right out of the room.

Kirsty and Rachel raced after him, with Sienna zooming alongside them. They saw him run into the makeup

room. It was empty now, except for some hairbrushes and makeup.

Kirsty shut the door behind them and carefully looked around. There weren't many places to hide. There were no boxes on the floor, or closets to duck into. There were just the three large swivel chairs where the girls had their hair done earlier. All three chairs had their backs to Sienna and the girls.

"He must be in one of those chairs,"
Kirsty mouthed to the others.

Rachel nodded thoughtfully. Then

she took a deep breath,
grabbed hold of the
closest chair, and
swung it around.
Whizz! The chair
spun around on its
base, but it was empty.

Kirsty spun the second chair to face
them, but that was
empty, too. She
and Rachel
looked at each
other. The goblin
had to be hiding
in the third chair!

Kirsty grinned. "Sienna, could you use
some fairy magic to spin that chair
around really, really fast?" she whispered.

Sienna gave a low giggle and nodded.
She waved her wand at the third chair,
and a flood of bright
pink sparkles
whirled out
of the tip.
The chair
suddenly
began to spin
faster and
faster and faster,
until it was a blur in
front of them.
Now the girls could see that the goblin
was indeed in the chair, and he was
getting awfully dizzy!

"Stop! I feel sick," he moaned. "Let me off!"

Sienna waved her wand again. The chair slowed down and came to a stop. The goblin looked very pale as he stumbled out of the chair. He swayed from side to side and then tried to run past the girls to the door. Unfortunately for the goblin, he was so dizzy that he couldn't go in a straight line. He was wobbling all over the place!

It was easy for Kirsty to grab the flag from his fingers. "I'll take that, thank you very much!" she cried triumphantly. Then she raised her hand and held the Saturday flag well out of the goblin's reach.

Saturday Fashion Fun!

Kirsty handed the flag to Sienna. The fairy waved her wand over it, shrinking it to its usual Fairyland size.

"Thank you," Sienna said. Then she shook her finger at the goblin. "You're lucky I don't tell Jack Frost what you've been up to!"

The goblin stuck out his bottom lip in a

childish pout. He tried to storm off, but he was still so dizzy that he bumped into one of the makeup stands and sent everything flying! "*Achoo!*" He sneezed, and a cloud of face powder filled the air.

The girls couldn't help giggling as the goblin stomped away, dusty with powder and sneezing miserably.

"Good job, girls," Sienna said happily. She waved her wand over the spilled powder, and it immediately vanished. All of the makeup brushes and hairspray bottles bounced up from where they had fallen. At once, they neatly arranged themselves back on the stand. The jar of face powder was instantly full again, and its lid twisted itself tightly closed. "That's better," Sienna said. She grinned at the girls. "And now you two should get dressed in your final outfits!"

"Oh, yes," Rachel cried, heading for the door. "I'd almost forgotten about the show!"

Back in the dressing room, the girls quickly pulled on their outfits. They wore sparkly tops with jeans and pretty pink-and-white sneakers. Sienna helpfully waved her wand to tie the shoelaces as soon as the girls put them on.

"Thanks, Sienna." Kirsty smiled, checking her hair in the mirror.

"Good luck," Sienna replied. "I'll go back to Fairyland now to charge up my wand. Hopefully, I'll be back with some Saturday Fun Day magic very soon!"

Kirsty and Rachel ran to the catwalk, and Susan and Caroline checked their outfits before they went on.

"You look wonderful," Caroline told them.

"Everyone's been great," Susan added, smiling at some of the other models nearby. "In fact, the whole show has been great!" Then the smile slipped from her face. "I just can't understand why the audience isn't having a better time."

Caroline nodded. "It is kind of disappointing," she admitted.

Rachel felt sorry for her cousin. It was
obvious that Caroline and Susan
had worked incredibly hard to
pull the whole fashion show
together. "Hopefully,
they'll love these last
outfits," she said
with a big smile. "I
know I do."

Caroline hugged
her. "Thanks,
Rachel," she said.
"Now you two had
better get ready.
You're on next!"

Kirsty and Rachel
went to their entrances and
stepped onto the stage when
Susan gave them their cue.

A party tune began to play, and a huge, sparkly disco ball started to spin above the catwalk. The glittery ball sent tiny colorful twinkles of light all over the audience. "Oooh!" people said in delight. Kirsty and Rachel couldn't help smiling at each other. This was more like it! "This is Sienna's magic. I'm sure of it," Rachel said happily.

61

The girls began dancing down the catwalk, and then Susan and Caroline ushered the other models onto the catwalk, too, to dance along behind them. It wasn't long before the audience was up on their feet, dancing and clapping, and having a fabulous time.

"All of a sudden, this feels like a party!" Kirsty cheered.

"Yes, thanks to you-know-who!"
Rachel replied. The girls glanced up to
see Sienna riding on the twirling disco
ball. The fairy was waving merrily at
them. Then Sienna blew them a kiss and
waved her wand. There was a loud pop,
and glittery confetti and streamers, in all
the colors of the rainbow, showered over
everyone.

A huge cheer went up from the models and audience. Everyone was having a wonderful, glittery time, and the *Gazette* photographer was taking lots of photos.

Sienna fluttered down, hidden within the confetti, to say a last goodbye. "Thanks again, girls," she said to Rachel and Kirsty. "I must go and do more of my Fun Day work. Enjoy yourselves, and good-bye!"

"Everyone's having lots of fun now, thanks to you!" Kirsty said, smiling.

"Yes, thanks, Sienna," Rachel agreed. "Good-bye!"

Sienna waved and disappeared in a whirl of pink sparkles.

The music ended a few minutes later, and the audience gave Caroline, Susan, and the models a standing ovation.

Rachel couldn't stop beaming. "The fashion show was a huge success," she whispered to Kirsty.

Kirsty nodded. "And now there's only one flag left to find!" she added happily.

THE FUN DAY FAIRIES

Six of the Fun Day Fairies have their
magical flags back. Can Rachel and
Kirsty find the final flag with some
help from

Sarah
the Sunday
Fairy?

Gobbling Goblin

"I can't believe it's Sunday already!" Kirsty Tate said, glancing at her best friend, Rachel Walker. They were in the Walkers' kitchen, wrapping sandwiches in plastic bags. "My mom and dad are coming to pick me up tonight," Kirsty added. "This week has gone so quickly!"

"Yes, it has," Rachel agreed. "That's because we've been busy looking for the fairies' Fun Day Flags!"

Just then, Mr. Walker hurried in, carrying a large straw picnic basket. Rachel stopped talking immediately and grinned at Kirsty. Nobody else knew that the two girls had a magical secret: they were friends with the fairies!

"Let's hurry up and pack the food, girls," said Mr. Walker, putting the picnic basket on the table. "We want to get an early start so we can make the most of this sunny weather."

"It was a wonderful idea to have a picnic at Windy Lake, Dad," Rachel said, as she popped a plastic container of potato salad into the basket.

"And all this food looks delicious,"

Kirsty added, looking at a large peach
pie.

"Put the pie and sandwiches in last, or
they'll get squished," Mr. Walker
suggested as the girls added bottles of
water to the basket. "Will you finish
packing while I get the car out of the
garage?"

Kirsty and Rachel nodded.

"We only have Sarah the Sunday
Fairy's flag left to find now," Rachel
said, when Mr. Walker had gone.

"Yes, but this is the last flag. So the
goblins will be even more determined to
find it first," Kirsty pointed out.

Come flutter by Butterfly Meadow!

Butterfly Meadow #1: Dazzle's First Day
Dazzle is a new butterfly, fresh out of her cocoon. She doesn't know how to fly, and she's all alone! But Butterfly Meadow could be just what Dazzle is looking for.

Butterfly Meadow #2: Twinkle Dives In
Twinkle is feisty, fun, and always up for an adventure. But the nearby pond holds much more excitement than she expected!